ROMAN
NEEDS A BATH

WRITTEN BY
S.K. PU'U

ILLUSTRATED BY
POTATO SAUCE

Dear Reader,

Did you know that you can get early access to cover reveals, character illustrations, upcoming releases, giveaways, and more before it's shared with everyone else on social media?

Join my Member's Only group and have immediate access to behind-the-scenes content on all my novels, writing resources, and more! You can find the link at the back of this book!

Thanks for reading and I hope you enjoy 'Roman Needs A Bath'.

S. K. Pru

If you enjoyed the book, please leave a review. Just go to my author page www.amazon.com/S-K-Puu/e/B08TRSFMWV.

I love connecting with my readers and want to know what you feel about my story. Plus the more reviews we have, the more readers will find the story. Writing for you is my dream! Thank you for making it possible.

Join S.K.Pu'u's Advance Reader list to receive bonus content and new release dates at www.zhenaloha.com/romannabcoloringbook

S.K. Pu'u Publishing
Macon, GA 31220
www.zhenaloha.com/skpuu

Publisher's Note: This is a work of fiction. Names, characters, places, and incidents are a product of the author's imagination. Locales and public names are sometimes used for atmospheric purposes. Any resemblance to actual people, living or dead, or to businesses, companies, events, institutions, or locales is completely coincidental.

Ordering Information: Special discounts are available on quantity purchases by corporations, associations, and others. For details, contact the publisher at the website above.

Macon / S.K. Pu'u — First Edition

ISBN 978-1-7363628-0-8

Printed in the United States of America

Made in the USA
Monee, IL
16 February 2022

90473089R00021